For my friend, agent and idol Marcia Wernick,
who always knows just what to ask for
E. C. K.

For Staci, who didn't even ask for Osbert, but loves him anyway
H. B. L.

First published 2004 by Walker Books Ltd
87 Vauxhall Walk, London SE11 5HJ

This edition produced 2004 for
The Book People Ltd, Hall Wood Avenue,
Haydock, St Helens WA11 9UL

2 4 6 8 10 9 7 5 3 1

Text © 2004 Elizabeth Cody Kimmel
Illustrations © 2004 H. B. Lewis

The right of Elizabeth Cody Kimmel and H. B. Lewis to be identified as
author and illustrator respectively of this work has been asserted
by them in accordance with the Copyright, Designs and Patents Act 1988

This book has been typeset in Colwell

Printed in China

British Library Cataloguing in Publication Data:
a catalogue record for this book
is available from the British Library

ISBN 0-7445-8571-6

www.walkerbooks.co.uk

My Penguin
Osbert

Elizabeth Cody Kimmel

illustrated by
H. B. Lewis

TED SMART

This year, I was very specific in my letter to Santa Claus.

We've had a few misunderstandings in the past.
For instance, last year I asked for a fire-engine-red
racing car with a detachable roof, a lightning bolt
on the side and retracting headlights.
And he did bring me one.

But it was only ten centimetres long.

And the year before I had really wanted
a trampoline. I wasn't sure how to spell it,
so in my letter I just sort of described
what I wanted.

Santa brought me a pogo stick.

So this year I was really, really careful. I wrote Santa a long letter and told him that I would like to have my own pet penguin. Not a stuffed penguin, but a real one, from Antarctica.

I told him my penguin should be thirty centimetres tall, white and black with a yellow beak, and his name should be Osbert. I included a drawing.

I put extra postage on the envelope and sent it off a whole month early.

Then I waited.

When Christmas morning came, I was the first one downstairs.

There he was!

He was black and white with a yellow beak, and exactly thirty centimetres tall.
He was moving
    and breathing
        and everything.

Around his neck was a tag.
It said:

HELLO
MY NAME IS:
OSBERT

Santa had got it right!

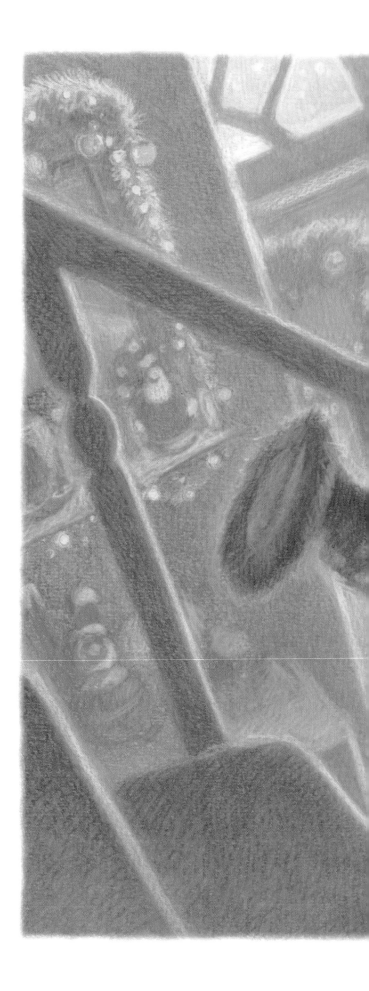

I wanted Osbert to meet everybody.
I wanted to take him to my room.
Plus, I wanted to open my other presents.

But Osbert really wanted to go outside
and play.

It was pretty cold out, and kind of windy
too. There was deep snow on the ground,
and no sun.

But I had asked for Osbert,
and now I had him.

So we went outside.

We played powder slide and wreck the igloo.

We had snowball fights and made ice penguins.

We escaped from the jaws of imaginary leopard seals.

Osbert wanted to go swimming, but I explained
how that wasn't possible. So we sang some of the
old penguin songs instead.

That night I was ready to go straight to bed. We'd had such a big day. But Osbert wanted to have a bath.

He filled the bathtub to the very top and we got in. Osbert unwrapped all the bars of soap and floated them around like icebergs.

After a while I had prune fingers, and my skin itched from all the soap.

But I had asked for Osbert, and now I had him.

And Osbert liked playing in a cold bath.

The next morning, Mum said she'd make ANYTHING I wanted for breakfast.

When I closed my eyes, I saw a stack of chocolate-chip waffles with hot syrup, a plate piled high with fried sausages and a jug of freshly squeezed mango juice.

But Osbert doesn't like rich food, and he doesn't like hot food, and he doesn't like sweet food.

Osbert wanted chilled herring with seaweed jam for breakfast.

So that's what we had.

After breakfast it was my turn to clear up. So I did the dishes and went upstairs to tidy my room.

When I came back down, I saw that Osbert had been working too. He had built an entire ice village out of icicles, frozen leftovers and tubs of ice cream from the freezer.

And now it was *all* melting.

Osbert, of course, couldn't hold a cloth in his flippers.

But I had asked for Osbert, and now I had him.

So I cleaned up the mess myself.

That afternoon, when Osbert was watching
the weather channel on cable TV,
I secretly wrote Santa another letter:

Dear Santa,

How are you and Mrs Claus? We are fine.

Thank you for the great penguin, called
Osbert. We have cold baths together and eat
herring and seaweed jam for breakfast.

I am getting used to spending all day
in the snow.

Plus, it turned out I didn't have frostbite after
all.

your friend,
Joe

P.S. One more thing, Santa. If you feel like maybe
I should have asked for a different present,
and you want to swap, that would be OK.

And while Osbert was leafing through
a snow-globe catalogue, I sneaked out and
posted the letter:

A few days later, I woke up to find a parcel at the foot of my bed. There was a label with my name on it, signed

Santa

Inside the box was a red sweater and two free tickets to the grand opening of Antarctic World at the zoo.

After Osbert had made a shrimp sculpture out of the wrapping paper, he wanted to go there straight away. But he didn't want to take the bus. The zoo was a long way away, but I had asked for Osbert, and now I had him.

So we walked.

When we got to Antarctic World, Osbert headed straight for the Penguin Palace.

There was a huge snowy hill with an ice slide leading down to a big pool. There were leopard seals painted on the walls. Tiny bergs of real ice were floating in the water.

And then a door opened in the wall and a man came out and started tossing herring to all the penguins.

When it was closing time, I told Osbert we had to leave.

He waddled over to me, but I knew he felt at home in the Penguin Palace. It had everything he needed.

Osbert was the first Christmas present Santa ever gave me that I really wanted. I had asked for Osbert, and I had been given him.

But Osbert needed ice slides and leopard seals and plenty of herring. I asked him if he would be happier living at the Penguin Palace. Osbert looked into my eyes. And then he nodded.

It's a little lonely at home without Osbert. And my new sweater itches my neck a little bit, right under my chin.

But it's nice to be warm. And I had chocolate-chip waffles for breakfast!

Next Saturday is Children Visit Free Day at Antarctic World. I don't have the bus fare but I know how to walk there. I'll wear my red sweater so Osbert will be sure to recognize me.

And next Christmas is only eleven months away!

I've thought about it a lot, and I already know what I want.

I'm sure I can't get into too much trouble with just one helicopter!